Tiny Puppies

Written by V.C. Graham
Illustrated by Marina Fedotova

Published by Sequoia Children's Publishing,
an imprint of Phoenix International Publications, Inc.

8501 West Higgins Road, Suite 790   59 Gloucester Place
Chicago, Illinois 60631   London W1U 8JJ

Sequoia Children's Publishing and associated logo are trademarks and/or
registered trademarks of Phoenix International Publications, Inc.
© 2018 Phoenix International Publications, Inc.

www.sequoiakidsbooks.com

10 9 8 7 6 5 4 3 2 1

ISBN 978-1-64269-044-6

1 tiny puppy
    digs a wee hole.

2 tiny puppies
splash in their bowl.

3 tiny puppies
explore an old shoe.

4 tiny puppies
check out the view.

5 tiny puppies chase butterflies.

6 tiny puppies
like a surprise.

7 tiny puppies have
full little tummies.

8 tiny puppies know
to go on the funnies.

9 tiny puppies
turn off the light.

10 tiny puppies
kiss Mama good night.